CONTENTS

CHAPTER 1

HIKING

"Joseph Anthony Keys, turn off your phone and listen to what your father and I are trying to tell you," Mum said from the front seat of the family car. "We'll be at Shenandoah National Park soon."

"OK, OK," twelve-year-old Joseph grumbled. He rolled his eyes at his friend on the other end of the video call. "Rob, I have to hang up. My parents are forcing me to go hiking and camping with them on some sort of trail."

"The Appalachian Trail, Joseph," Mum retorted.

Rob looked surprised. "The Appalachian Trail? That sounds so cool!"

Joseph snorted. "What's so cool about it? I'm going to miss your birthday party because we have to go and walk around in the woods and do some bird-watching."

"This holiday is more than just looking at birds," Dad corrected as he navigated down the motorway. "It's about us spending time together, learning and enjoying the wonders of nature."

"I can enjoy the wonders of nature in our garden," Joseph joked. "Couldn't we have just roasted some marshmallows there?"

"That's it, hang up right now, or I'm taking your phone away for the rest of the holiday!" Mum said. "You've already missed so much of the wonderful scenery because you've been on your phone for the entire drive."

Joseph sighed. They'd been in the car for hours – ever since leaving home at the crack of dawn. The last thing he wanted to do was go on a trip through the wilderness. It would be even worse if he had to do it without his phone.

"Speak to you later, Rob," Joseph muttered.

"Later!" Rob said as he ended the call.

Joseph put his phone away and sighed again. "I don't see what the big deal is about walking in the woods. It's just a load of trees and insects out there. We could be doing something much more interesting instead. Why this?"

"The great outdoors is more than just trees and insects," Mum said. "And hiking can be more dangerous than you think. You need to pay attention or you could put yourself at serious risk."

"I doubt it," Joseph muttered under his breath.

"What was that?" Dad said.

"Nothing," Joseph said, turning to stare out of the window. As far as he was concerned, the sooner this trip was over, the better.

CHAPTER 2

WHAT'S THE BIG DEAL?

Three hours later, the Keys family finally arrived at Shenandoah National Park. Dad parked the car, and everyone climbed out.

Joseph stood and stretched his legs. He was happy be out of the car, even if they did seem to be in the middle of nowhere.

Mum and Dad grabbed the luggage. Joseph struggled to put on his rucksack. It was harder than he'd expected.

"Why do they make these things so difficult to put on?" he whined.

"We tried to show you how to put it

on before we left home, but you couldn't be bothered," Dad said.

"I was busy," Joseph grumbled.

"Yes, too busy to even pack your own bag," Mum retorted. "I had to do it for you. It would be nice if you could try and appreciate this holiday."

"You need to adjust your attitude," Dad said. "You're too attached to your phone. Perhaps if you unplugged sometimes you'd enjoy yourself and see the health benefits."

Joseph didn't say anything. He was sick of his parents always going on at him about being on his phone. How else was he supposed to talk to his friends?

After a few more minutes of struggling with the straps, Joseph finally managed to get his rucksack on. It was so heavy. Together, he and his parents walked over to the rangers' office. As they entered, a uniformed man greeted them.

"Good afternoon!" he said, smiling at them. "I'm Ranger James. Welcome to Shenandoah National Park, one part of the massive Appalachian Trail. Have you come to check in?"

"Yes," said Joseph's dad. "We're the Keys family."

"Ah, I've been expecting you. You'll be cabin sharing with the Sharma family," Ranger James said. "Follow me, and I'll introduce you to them."

Joseph rolled his eyes. *We have to share a cabin with another family? Ugh. Great, more people I don't want to be around.*

Ranger James led Joseph and his parents out of the office and down a winding, rutted mud path. Lush chestnut trees lined it.

As they walked, Joseph saw a spider sitting in the middle of a massive web. The creature sat suspended between two of the chestnut trees.

Ugh, I hate spiders, Joseph thought with a shiver. Just seeing a spider made him itch uncomfortably.

A few moments later, they arrived at the cabin. Joseph looked at the run-down living quarters and sighed. The covered front porch housed some dusty old rocking chairs, and an outdoor fireplace had been set up a metre away. The cabin was definitely big enough for two families, but not big enough for Joseph to have space for himself.

Hopefully we'll have electricity, he thought.

"Here we are," Ranger James said. "Cabin fifteen." He opened the door to the cabin. Inside, another family was already settling in.

"Keys family, meet the Sharmas," Ranger James said. "I'm sure you're all tired from your journeys, but there's a chance we might have a storm tomorrow on your group hike. Let's discuss tips for hiking in bad weather when you've finished settling in."

As Joseph's parents greeted the other adults, a girl who looked about Joseph's age walked over.

"Hi," she said. "I'm Nadia."

"Nice to meet you," Joseph replied. "I'm Joseph. Did your parents drag you on this trip, too?"

Nadia shook her head. "It was actually my idea," she said. "This is my fourth hiking holiday, but I've never been on the trail before. How about you? Do you love hiking, too?"

Great, Joseph thought. *Another outdoor enthusiast.*

He shook his head. "No. But I don't have much of a choice, do I?"

Before Nadia could respond, Ranger James addressed the group again.

"You're all scheduled to go on a group hike on the trail tomorrow," he said, "so make sure you use your maps to stay on the safe paths."

I'd rather stay off all *paths*, Joseph thought. He resisted the urge to roll his eyes.

"It's up to your group if you want to do an up-and-back or camp overnight on the trail," the ranger continued. He studied both families. "Does everyone here know what 'up-and-back' means?"

Nadia put her hand up. "It's when you turn around and retrace your steps, heading back to where you started, on a hike," she replied.

"That's right!" said Ranger James. "You should also be prepared tomorrow if thunderstorms roll in while you're on the trail. Make sure you have the essentials: water, poncho, snacks, torch, first-aid kit and your tent."

"Can't we just come back if it rains?" Joseph asked. "Or use our phones to call for help?"

Ranger James nodded. "Some people enjoy the experience of camping in the rain, but if the storms are really bad, I would suggest coming back to your cabin," he said. "But as for the second part of your question, there's no mobile phone reception out on the trail. Using your phone out there is a waste of time."

Joseph's mother turned towards him and winked. "Did you hear that, Joseph? You'll have to live without your phone tomorrow."

Joseph shrugged. "We're only walking through the woods," he said. "I think I'll survive."

CHAPTER 3

WRONG TURN

The next day, the two families woke up
early. Everyone except Joseph seemed eager
for the group hike on the Appalachian Trail.
Everyone filled their rucksacks and set off
through the oak-hickory forest. The adults
walked together at the front, while Joseph
and Nadia brought up the rear.

The group walked past clusters of
colourful mushrooms and patches of moss
that grew on the trees. Massive rocks lay on
the trail. Ferns and freshwater plants lined
the route. The leaves from the red oaks in
the forest glistened in the sun.

Everyone seemed impressed by the beauty of the trail. Joseph, however, was not pleased. Thirty minutes into the three-hour hike, he just wanted to go home.

"Does anyone want to guess how many states the Appalachian Trail runs through?" Mr Sharma called back from the front of the group.

The parents turned and looked at Joseph and Nadia. Joseph shrugged his shoulders.

"Technically, the Appalachian Trail cuts through as many as fourteen states from start to finish," Nadia piped up.

"I should have guessed that you would know the answer," Joseph muttered.

"When I was younger, my dad took me and the entire family hiking," Joseph's dad said loudly. "We loved it so much. It was a tradition that I wanted to continue with our family. I can't believe I've waited so long to do it."

"That's very sweet," said Mrs Sharma.

The families continued along the trail. As the adults chatted, they slowly pulled ahead of the children.

Nadia studied the ground. "Watch your step, Joseph," she said. "There are a lot of roots on this part of the path."

Joseph didn't reply. At first Nadia thought he was just being rude. But when she looked up, she found him sitting on a log at the side of the trail, picking fungus off it.

"Come on, Joseph, we should catch up with our parents," Nadia said, walking over. The adults had disappeared around a bend in the trail. "Joseph?"

"Ugh, I don't want to be here at all. I hate hiking," Joseph grumbled.

"How can you hate something you've never tried? Give it a chance. Hiking can be a lot of fun," said Nadia.

"That's easy for you to say. You like this sort of thing. I got dragged here – and I'm missing out on being with my friends because of it. Just leave me alone," Joseph growled.

Nadia glared at him. "Fine. Stay here then." She turned and walked away.

"I will!" Joseph replied. He huffed, pleased to be left alone. But a moment later, there was a rustling noise in the brush.

What was that? Joseph thought. *Who's there?*

Suddenly a squirrel leapt from the brush and bounced off Joseph's head. Joseph panicked. He jumped up from the log and raced after Nadia. The squirrel chased after him.

"Wait for me!" Joseph called. He ran towards – and quickly past – Nadia. There was a fork in the trail up ahead, and he veered left.

"Slow down!" Nadia shouted. She watched

in shock as the squirrel continued its pursuit of Joseph. "You're going down the wrong path! Our parents went this way!"

Joseph didn't listen. With a sigh, Nadia ran after him. She was focussing so hard on catching up with him that she didn't look where she was going.

Before she knew it, Nadia tripped on a root. She slid off the narrow trail and tumbled down a large, sloped hill. She fell down a steep incline covered in ferns and grass. As she fell, Nadia saw Joseph, lying very still at the bottom of the hill.

CHAPTER 4

WHAT ARE WE GOING TO DO?

At the bottom of the hill, Nadia climbed to her feet. "Are you OK?" she asked Joseph. She walked over and checked him for injuries.

Joseph winced as she poked and prodded, but luckily, nothing seemed broken. He'd survived with just a few minor scratches.

"No, I'm not OK," Joseph snapped. "A wild animal tried to eat me–"

"Oh, you mean the squirrel that was chasing you down that path?" Nadia said, rolling her eyes. She brushed the mud off her clothes and removed her rucksack to make sure everything was still intact.

Joseph glared at her as he stood up. "It's not my fault. I tripped over a stupid root," he argued.

"It is your fault," Nadia said. "If you'd stayed with the group, we wouldn't be in this situation. Now our parents have no idea where we are."

"We just have to call for help," Joseph said. He pulled his smartphone from his pocket. "Come on, connect! Why can't I get a signal out here?" He held his phone in the air.

"The ranger told us yesterday that our phones wouldn't work out here," said Nadia. "Were you listening?"

Joseph didn't reply. "Mum! Dad! Can anyone hear me?" he shouted.

"We're too far off the trail. Our parents can't hear us," Nadia said.

"Let's climb back up the hill then," Joseph said.

Nadia pointed at the hill. "There's no way we can climb back up. It's too steep," she said.

She was right, Joseph realized. The hill they'd fallen down *was* steep and covered in slippy grass. There was nowhere along the fern-covered incline to get a grip or foothold. It seemed to stretch on like that forever.

Suddenly thunder rattled and the clouds began to roll in. Nadia and Joseph looked up. Raindrops started to slowly fall.

Nadia pulled out her poncho and put it on. Joseph struggled to take off his rucksack so he could check the contents. He realized he had no idea what was in there.

"Where is it? Where's my rain thingy?" Joseph said.

"Do you mean your poncho?" Nadia said.

"I must have one! This is the worst day of my life! I have no idea what I'm doing out here." Joseph continued to panic.

Nadia tried to calm him. "Panicking isn't going to help you find your poncho. Step back, take a deep breath and I'll look for it."

"OK. OK," Joseph said. He handed Nadia his bag and forced himself to take a deep breath.

What are we going to do? How are we going to find our parents? How are we going to get back to our cabin? he thought. *I just want to go home!*

Nadia found Joseph's poncho and threw it to him. He quickly put it on.

"Thanks," he said. "What shall we do now?"

Nadia looked up at the sky, which was now dark with storm clouds. The rain was starting to come down more steadily.

"We're going to have to pitch a tent," she said. "This storm is going to be here for a while."

CHAPTER 5

AN UNEXPECTED GUEST

Nadia and Joseph both dug through their rucksacks. They each had a tent, but Joseph's was larger.

"Let's just pitch yours," Nadia said. "It's big enough for both of us. There's no need to put mine up, too."

Joseph didn't know enough to argue, so he just nodded in agreement. Nadia prepared the poles as Joseph unrolled the tent. He struggled to insert the metal tubes into the tent and lock them in place, but with Nadia's help, he started to get the hang of it.

Wow, she really knows her stuff, Joseph thought as he watched Nadia work quickly and efficiently. *I'm lucky she's here. I'd have no idea what to do on my own.*

After thirty minutes, the tent was ready. Just in time, too – the rain had turned into a torrential downpour. The two crouched down and hurried inside the temporary shelter.

Nadia took her heat lamp from her rucksack. She turned it on and put it in the middle of the tent.

"This will give us light and keep us warm," she said.

"There are some small hooks in the corner. Let's put our ponchos there," Joseph suggested.

"Good idea. We'll put our rucksacks over there so they can dry off, too," said Nadia. "Your parents got you a great tent."

"Yes, I suppose they did," Joseph said, glancing around. It was a blue tent, big enough for at least three people. The curved roof was almost tall enough for Joseph and Nadia to stand up in the middle. "That must be why my rucksack was so heavy."

Nadia unrolled their sleeping bags. Joseph dug through his rucksack and pulled out some flapjacks made with almonds, cashews, cranberries and pumpkin seeds.

After taking one, he handed them to Nadia. It was the least he could do after Nadia had helped them get out of the rain.

They snacked silently for a while. Eventually Joseph said, "I'm sorry about how I acted on the trail. I didn't mean to get us into this mess. Or act like such an idiot. I just didn't want to go on this trip. It's my fault we're lost."

"We'll find a way back," Nadia said as she munched on some flapjack.

With her other hand, she pulled a sandwhich bag out of her back pocket. "Here, when you've finished with your flapjack, put the wrapper in this. It's called a bear bag. It seals the smell of food, so wild animals won't be tempted over to us."

"Oh. Thanks." Joseph took the bag.

"This storm is probably going to last through the night. We should rest here until morning," said Nadia. "Then we'll look at our maps and try to work out how to get back."

Suddenly there was a noise outside the tent – a low scratching followed by a growl. Whatever it was sounded different from the rain or thunder.

"Let's zip up the tent opening," said Nadia, glancing in that direction. Even she looked a little bit nervous.

"Yes, you should do that," Joseph agreed.

"Me?" Nadia said. "It's your tent!"

"I don't want whatever's out there to get me!" Joseph said.

"Me neither!" Nadia shouted. Taking a deep breath, she exhaled. "OK. Let's just close it together."

Joseph and Nadia looked at each other. Together they slowly approached the tent opening. As they were about to reach for the zipper, lightning flashed. Whatever was outside burst into the tent and jumped on Nadia!

"Get it off of me!" Nadia screamed.

Joseph started laughing when he realized what they'd been so scared of: a Jack Russell terrier, licking Nadia's face.

"It's just a dog," Joseph said. He grabbed the dog's harness and pulled it off Nadia. "He's probably hungry and lost, just like us."

Joseph pulled the soaking-wet dog over to the heat lamp to help him dry off. Nadia got a wipe from her rucksack and wiped the dog's slobber off her face.

"He's got a collar and tags," she said. "What's his name?"

Joseph checked the dog's collar. "Colt. Welcome to the team, Colt," he said. He rubbed the dog's head. Colt wagged his tail.

Outside, loud cracks of thunder and lightning continued to crash all around. After one particularly loud *boom,* an animal howled. It didn't sound far away.

"What do you think that howling noise was?" Nadia asked.

Joseph looked worried. The tent suddenly seemed less safe and secure.

"I don't know," he said. "And I don't want to find out."

CHAPTER 6

SLEEPLESS NIGHT

In the middle of the night, the rain and thunder roared. The wind from the storm rattled the tent.

The heat lamp kept them warm, but Joseph couldn't sleep, even with Colt and Nadia in the tent. Instead, he closed his eyes and thought of all the things he should have done differently.

My parents are probably worried sick about me. I should have listened to them, he thought. *I should have listened to the ranger when we arrived. I should have taken this seriously.*

Joseph huddled deeper into his sleeping bag, wishing he was safe and sound with his family. Even the cabin sounded good at this point.

As he lay there, Joseph's stomach growled loudly. Flapjack hadn't been a very filling dinner.

I wish I was eating Mum's spaghetti bolognese, he thought. *I wish I was in my own bed.*

"I want to go home," Joseph whispered quietly.

"Same," Nadia said. "This tent is nice, but it's not a real bed."

Joseph hadn't realized she was awake, too. Somehow that made him feel better.

"Every time I think I hear something outside, it wakes me up," he admitted. "I wonder if our parents are out in this awful weather looking for us."

"We should both try to get some sleep," Nadia said. "Tomorrow, when it's light outside, we'll pull out our compasses and maps. We have to work out where we are and how to get back."

Joseph wished he shared Nadia's confidence.

Just then, lightning struck again, followed by another loud boom of thunder. Joseph crept even deeper into his sleeping bag. His fears, meanwhile, began to creep to the surface.

But what if we don't find our way back? he worried. *What do we do then?*

CHAPTER 7

A BIG MISTAKE

The next day, Joseph and Nadia woke up early. The rain had stopped, and it was time to pack up the tent and their supplies.

Nadia disconnected all the poles into smaller pieces and wrapped them together with Velcro tape. Joseph carefully folded the tent, then secured it using the tent belt straps.

Using a loose cord that was in his rucksack, Joseph made a makeshift lead for Colt. He attached it to the dog's harness.

"There you go," Joseph said. "Now you won't get lost again. We'll get you back to your family."

The dog let out a whine. He seemed as anxious as Joseph felt.

"Don't forget to put your flapjack in your bear bag," Nadia reminded him. She took a drink from her flask. "And check to see how much water you have left. I've finished mine."

"OK," said Joseph. He fed Colt a handful of snacks, then put them down for a second so he could check his flask and put on his rucksack. "I've finished my water, too."

"Well at least we're near a river," Nadia said. "We can fill up with fresh water."

The two of them and Colt walked to the edge of the river. Colt began to lap up some water.

"I think I'll go a little upstream," Joseph said. "I don't want any dog germs swimming into my flask."

Nadia and Joseph took a few steps away from Colt. Nadia was about to dip her flask into the water when Joseph paused.

"I know I don't know much about hiking and camping," he said, "but our science teacher was telling us that certain types of water can have bacteria in it. Is this water safe to drink?"

Nadia paused and placed her flask at her side. "You're right. I completely forgot about that." She rummaged through her rucksack. "I always carry a water filter in case of emergency. It filters out bacteria and other stuff when we drink from it."

Nadia pulled out what looked like a huge handheld straw. She frowned.

"Oh no, it's broken," she said. "It must have smashed when we fell down the hill."

Joseph took off his rucksack. "Let me check mine," he said. Moments later he pulled a massive straw out of his own rucksack. "This is what we need, isn't it?"

Nadia grinned. "Yes! You're a lifesaver, Joseph!"

"Thanks! It feels good to be helpful for a change," Joseph replied.

He handed Nadia the purifying straw first. She knelt down and dipped the straw in the water, taking a few big gulps.

"Oh, that's good," said Nadia. She handed the purifying straw to Joseph, and he took a few big sips as well.

When they'd finished drinking, Joseph stuck the purifier back in his bag. They might need it again.

After that, he and Nadia finished putting on their rucksacks. Then Nadia pulled a map of the trail from her pocket. She unfolded it so they could look at it together.

"What are these little triangles with numbers all over the map?" Joseph asked, studying the paper.

"They're markers that are placed around the woods and trails. If people get lost, they can look at a map, get their bearings and work out what they're close to," Nadia explained.

Joseph turned around and looked in the distance. "There's a sign a little way down the river," he exclaimed. "I'll be back in a second!"

He set off, and sure enough, about forty steps away, there was a marker attached to a pole in the ground.

Marker fifty-seven, Joseph said to himself. He quickly turned around and made his way back to Nadia. "We're near marker fifty-seven!" he announced.

Nadia looked over the map. "I've found it!" she said. "We can walk three miles south, along the hillside. That should lead us back to the path and take us just a few kilometres away from our cabin!"

"That's great!" Joseph said. He exhaled a sigh of relief.

But his relief didn't last long. Colt began to growl. The dog was worried about something.

"What's wrong, Colt?" Joseph asked.

He and Nadia looked up from their map, and at the same time, they both froze. There, blocking their path back to the cabin, was a baby black bear. It was eating Joseph's flapjack. Nadia looked alarmed. "I thought you put your flapjack in the bear bag!" she said quietly.

"I meant to!" Joseph whispered back. "But then we started talking about water straws and how to get out of here, and I got distracted."

The bear was just a cub, but even Joseph knew what that meant. Where there was a cub, there was probably a mother bear nearby.

Black bear mothers were very protective of their young.

Nadia took a deep breath, but her hands were shaking. "We have to stay calm," she said. "Do not panic."

Joseph didn't have time to panic before things went from bad to worse. A larger bear – probably the cub's mother – lumbered out of the trees.

Colt let out a whimper. Joseph wanted to whimper, too. They were in serious danger.

CHAPTER 8

BEWARE OF BEARS

"What shall we do?" Joseph asked.

Nadia kept her voice low. "I did some reading about bears in the area before we came on the trip," she said. "We have to stay calm. Start slowly walking backwards, away from the bears. Keep eye contact with them to see how they react. Do not run. Keep walking back until we're out of sight."

Leaning down, Nadia scooped Colt into her arms. That way he couldn't run off.

"OK," Joseph replied. "But they're blocking our way back. How are we going to get back now?"

"Let's work that out when we're away from the bears," Nadia said. They began to slowly walk backwards. "It's important to talk to them in a calm voice so the mum doesn't view us as a threat."

Joseph nodded. He was willing to do whatever Nadia said if it meant getting out of harm's way.

"Hi, bears," Nadia said. "Please have the flapjack. We hope you like it. We mean you no harm. Easy there. Easy now."

The mother bear stayed close to her cub. It was still happily rummaging through the bag of food. Joseph, Nadia and Colt crept backwards, staying close to the river, getting further and further away from the bears.

After a few minutes, they were around the bend, out of the bears' sight.

"Do you think we're OK now?" asked Joseph.

"I don't know," said Nadia. "The mother bear can probably still smell us. And bears have very good hearing. But if she wanted to chase us, she probably would've done it by now."

"You learned all this stuff about bears from that website?" Joseph asked. He was impressed.

"That, and I did a project on them for school a while ago," Nadia replied.

Joseph was tempted to stop and check the map to work out where they were going. But even though he could no longer see the bears, he heard a low, deep growl through the trees.

"What was that growl for?" asked Joseph.

"I don't know, but the further away we are from it, the better!" Nadia said.

Joseph nodded. The map would have to wait.

CHAPTER 9

HELP!

Joseph and Nadia kept moving until they'd put a safe distance between themselves and the bears. Only then did they stop to check the map.

"Let's keep heading north," Nadia said, studying the route. "There's a trail shelter that way."

Joseph nodded in agreement, and the kids and dog set off. Eventually they made their way back to the main trail. It had taken much longer than expected, but they'd avoided any more wild animal encounters.

"I can't wait until we get to the shelter," Nadia said as they walked side by side. "I love the outdoors, but this is too much for me. What's the first thing you're going to do when we get back to our parents?"

"Have a long shower," Joseph said with a laugh. "Then have a huge meal. Flapjack is fine, but I need some proper food."

"Same here," Nadia said as Colt began to bark. "I think Colt wants some proper food, too."

Joseph and Nadia laughed as they continued towards the shelter.

"Thanks again for helping me survive this," said Joseph. "I would have been lost out here without you."

"You helped, too," Nadia said. "I wouldn't have wanted to spend the night out here alone either."

"You wouldn't have had to if it wasn't for me," Joseph reminded her.

Nadia smiled. "That might be true. But think how much you've learned," she told him. "You managed to put up and put down a tent. And you had a working water filter."

"I suppose you're right," Joseph said. "Parts of it were even fun."

"It's OK to have fun in the great outdoors," Nadia agreed. "You just need to be aware and prepared, too."

After a few kilometres, they passed marker fifty-four. "Almost there!" said Nadia, taking the lead.

"That's great, I can't wait to–" Joseph's voice suddenly cut off. He and Colt both yelped as they fell.

"Joseph?" Nadia said, turning around.

Where Joseph and Colt had been moments before was a hole about a metre wide. It was hidden from sight by the taller grass along the trail.

"Down here! We're down here!" Joseph shouted. Colt barked and whimpered.

Nadia stared down into the hole. From up above, it seemed extremely deep. She could just about make out Joseph and the dog at the bottom of it.

"Are you OK?" Nadia called.

"I don't know," Joseph called up to her. "My ankle hurts a bit. I broke Colt's fall, so he's OK."

"Can you climb out?" asked Nadia.

Joseph stood up slowly. His ankle was throbbing, and the hole was damp and muddy. He tried to get a grip on the thin roots along the wall, but it was too slippery. Every step he took sent him sliding back to the bottom.

"I can't climb up. It's too slippery," he called up. "Is there any rope in your rucksack?"

"Hold on!" Nadia said.

She took off her rucksack and pulled some rope from one of the compartments. She threw one end down the hole, but it was too short.

"This isn't going to work," Nadia said, frustrated. "Listen, the shelter isn't that far away. I'm going to go and get some help. Hold on. I promise I'll be back!"

"Be careful!" Joseph shouted.

Nadia ran in the direction of the shelter. As she sprinted along the grassy trail, she kept an eye out for any other holes. She didn't want to end up like Joseph.

Suddenly, over the hill she spotted a small wooden cabin with windows and an overhanging roof. The shelter!

Nadia ran even faster to get to it. Within moments, she was at the front door and quickly opened it.

A ranger looked up from her desk as Nadia burst in. "Are you OK?" the ranger asked. "What's wrong?"

Nadia panted for breath. "My friend and I got lost yesterday," she said. "We were on our way here when he and our dog fell into a big hole! I think he's hurt his ankle really badly!"

The ranger shook her head. "Those old trap holes are everywhere. Hunters used to use them to trap animals. Every time we think we've filled them all, another one pops up. Don't worry, we'll get your friend and your dog out of there."

The ranger gathered her crew. They grabbed a rope ladder and a first-aid kit.

"Show us where your friend is," the ranger said.

"Follow me!" said Nadia.

* * *

Joseph and Colt sat in the hole, waiting. "I hope Nadia's OK," Joseph said, looking at Colt. "What if she gets trapped, too? Then who's going to rescue us?"

Colt began to lick Joseph's face. "OK, OK, I'll stop worrying," he said.

Suddenly Joseph heard a rustle of footsteps and people talking. Then he heard Nadia's voice. "Hold on, Joseph!" she called.

A moment later, a rope ladder fell in front of Joseph and Colt.

"Are you OK?" another voice called. Joseph looked up to see a ranger peering down into the hole from above.

"I think so. But I can't put a lot of pressure of my left ankle," said Joseph.

"That's OK, we'll come down and get you out of there," the ranger replied.

"I told you I'd be back!" Nadia shouted.

The rangers used spikes to secure the rope ladder. Then the lead ranger went down to rescue Joseph and Colt.

"Thank you so much for helping us," said Joseph when he and Colt were back up on the trail.

"That's what we're here for," the ranger replied. "Now tell me, how did you two end up out here all alone?"

Joseph and Nadia exchanged a look. "It's a long story," they said in unison.

CHAPTER 10

SAFE AND SOUND

Inside the ranger's office, Joseph's and Nadia's parents waited for their children. As the door opened, they jumped up. Nadia and Colt walked in with Joseph limping behind them.

"Nadia, you're OK! Thank goodness!" Nadia's mother exclaimed. Her parents swept her up in a big hug. "We're so glad you're OK. We had search parties looking all over for you two!"

"We'll arrange for a doctor to look at Joseph's ankle," the ranger said. "He may have a bad sprain."

Joseph's parents held tightly onto their son.

"Mum, Mum, I can't breathe. You're hugging me too tight," Joseph said.

Joseph's mum eased off a bit. His dad gave him a big hug. "We were so worried. What happened?" he asked. "And where did you find this dog?"

"This is Colt," said Joseph. "We found him the first night that we got lost and–"

Before Joseph could finish, Colt bolted out of the office.

"Where's he going?" Joseph said.

He limped back out of the office. Nadia and their parents followed. Outside, a little girl and her family surrounded Colt.

"Colt! There you are! I've been so worried!" The little girl held Colt close, then turned to Joseph and Nadia. "Are you the ones who found my dog?"

"Yes," said Joseph.

"Colt is really clever," said Nadia. "He alerted us to the bears!"

"Bears?" Joseph's mother repeated.

"I'll explain everything later," Joseph said, "but first I owe you and Dad an apology. It was my attitude and behaviour that got Nadia and me into this mess. The wilderness is not a joke, and the trail can be dangerous if you're not paying attention."

"I wish it hadn't taken getting lost on the trail to teach you that lesson, but I'm glad you understand now," Dad said. "But more than anything, I'm just happy that you're OK."

"Joseph helped us find a way back," Nadia chimed in. "And he's learned how to put up a tent. And he saved us from dehydration with his water filter!"

Joseph blushed. "I suppose I did learn something," he said.

"Can we get something to eat?" said Nadia. "We're starving! All we've had to eat is flapjack."

"After that, if my ankle is OK, can we walk the actual trail tomorrow?" said Joseph. "I really want to learn more about it. Even though we've had a bit of an adventure, I think I'm starting to like the outdoors."

Joseph's parents looked shocked. "Really?" Mum said.

Joseph nodded. "But for now, can Nadia and I have some proper food, please?"

AUTHOR BIO

Shawn Pryor is the creator and co-writer of the all-ages graphic novel mystery series Cash & Carrie, writer of *Kentucky Kaiju* and writer and co-creator of the 2019 GLYPH-nominated football/drama series Force. He is also the author of the Jake Maddox Sports Stories title *Diamond Double Play*. In his spare time, Shawn enjoys reading, cooking, listening to music and talking about why Zack from the *Mighty Morphin Power Rangers* is the greatest superhero of all time.

ILLUSTRATOR BIO

Alan Brown is an illustrator working in children's books and comics. His love of art started as a young boy, when he had unlimited access to comics at his gran's sweetie shop. These days, he can be found at his desk, illustrating with help from his two sons and dog.

GLOSSARY

bacteria very small living things that exist all around you and inside you; some bacteria cause disease

canteen small metal container for holding water

dehydration life-threatening medical condition caused by a lack of water

enthusiast person who is very excited about or interested in something

filter device that cleans liquids or gases as they pass through it

incline slanting surface

lush covered with a thick growth of healthy plants

ranger person in charge of a park or forest

shelter safe, covered place

steep having a very sharp slope

torrential coming in a large, fast stream

unison at exactly the same time

DISCUSSION QUESTIONS

1. Imagine you and your family are going hiking on the Appalachian Trail. Describe one thing you would most like to see or do? Talk about what it is and why it's important to you.

2. Joseph and Nadia were lucky to escape from the danger of the black bear and her cub while making their way back to camp. What other types of scary situations do you think could happen while hiking? Talk about some possible dangers.

3. In this story, Joseph struggles to put up the tent until Nadia gives him a hand. Think about something you struggled to accomplish until you received help from someone else. Talk about what it was, who helped you and how the help made a difference.

WRITING PROMPTS

1. Have you ever been on a hiking or camping trip? Describe your experience in a few paragraphs. If you haven't done either of these things, describe what you would like to do during your hiking or camping trip.

2. It can be interesting to think about a story from a different point of view. Try writing Chapter 5 from Colt the dog's point of view. What was Colt thinking about when he jumped inside Joseph and Nadia's tent?

3. Joseph's parents wanted him to spend less time on his phone and more time enjoying the great outdoors. How do you think Joseph felt about that at the start of the story compared to the end? Write a few paragraphs explaining how his attitude changed after his hiking experience.

THAT'S A LOT OF HIKING

The Appalachian Trail is more than three thousand kilometres long and runs across the eastern United States. It is the longest hiking path in the world. It travels through fourteen US states: Georgia, North Carolina, Tennessee, Virginia, West Virginia, Maryland, Pennsylvania, New Jersey, New York, Connecticut, Massachusetts, Vermont, New Hampshire and Maine.

Nearly fifteen thousand people have hiked the entire Appalachian Trail, which can take between five and seven months to complete. The elevation changes along the trail making completing the hike the same as climbing Mount Everest sixteen times! (The summit of Mount Everest is 8,848 metres.)

According to the Appalachian Mountain Club, the Appalachian Trail crosses a road every 6.5 kilometres. Along these roads are many small mountain communities, which can make it easier to find your way back to civilization. In some areas, the Appalachian Trail runs straight through many towns or passes within a few kilometres of other towns.

WHAT ABOUT THE BEARS?

Black bears live and pass through almost all parts of the Appalachian Trail. Bears usually avoid people, so an encounter is unlikely. But if you're in black bear country, it's better to travel in a group. (You shouldn't move through a bear's habitat silently or alone.)

If you do happen to come across a black bear, know what to do. Here are a few tips:

- Keep a safe distance. Give the bear as much space as possible. If you can, go back the way you came. If you have to continue, give the bear a lot of space.

- Identify yourself by speaking calmly and firmly so the bear knows you are a human, not prey.

- Stay calm. Stand your ground but slowly wave your arms in the air. This will make you appear larger and more intimidating.

- Walk, don't run and keep your eyes on the bear so you can see how it's reacting.

THE FUN DOESN'T STOP HERE!

You can find more of your favourite characters and exciting Sport Stories at:

www.raintree.co.uk